D0563779

WITHDRAWN

VOLCANO!

A *SURVIVE!* Story

BY JAKE MADDOX

illustrated by Sean Tiffany

text by Eric Stevens

STONE ARCH BOOKS
www.stonearchbooks.com

Impact Books are published by Stone Arch Books
151 Good Counsel Drive, P.O. Box 669
Mankato, Minnesota 56002
www.stonearchbooks.com

Library of Congress Cataloging-in-Publication Data
Maddox, Jake.
    Volcano / by Jake Maddox; illustrated by Sean Tiffany.
    p. cm. — (Impact Books. A Jake Maddox Sports Story)
    ISBN 978-1-4342-1208-5 (library binding)
    ISBN 978-1-4342-1407-2 (pbk.)
    [1. Camping—Fiction. 2. Volcanoes—Fiction. 3. Wilderness
survival—Fiction. 4. Survival—Fiction.] I. Tiffany, Sean, ill. II. Title.
PZ7.M25643Vo 2009
[Fic]—dc22   2008031963

Summary:
It was supposed to be a fun camping trip. Tom and Kevin had been
looking forward to it all summer. But when the long-dormant volcano
erupts, their fun trip vanishes, replaced by a mad dash for survival. Tom
and Kevin have to use their smarts to outrun the lava spilling madly
from the volcano's peak.

Creative Director: Heather Kindseth
Graphic Designer: Carla Zetina-Yglesias

1 2 3 4 5 6 14 13 12 11 10 09

Printed in the United States of America

TABLE OF CONTENTS

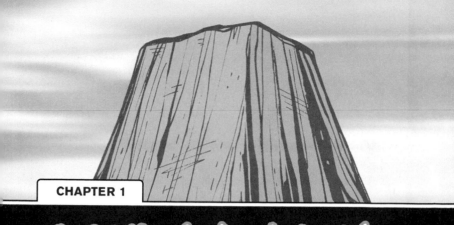

CHAPTER 1

A REAL, LIVE VOLCANO

An old blue pickup truck bounced along a quiet dirt road. Tall pines towered all around, and a cool rain was falling like mist.

A raven hopped away from the side of the road as the truck passed. Two deer lifted their heads from some breakfast to watch the truck go by.

The man driving smiled slightly as he guided the truck. To his right, two boys talked and laughed, excited.

"So you and your dad take this trip every year?" asked the boy sitting by the window.

The other boy, squished between his father and his friend, nodded. "Yup," he said. "Every fall for the seven days before school starts up again."

"Tom's right," said the driver. "In fact, did you know you're first person we ever brought along, Kevin?"

"Really?" asked Kevin, the boy by the window. "It's always been just you two before?"

Tom and his father nodded. "That's right," Tom's dad said.

"Yup," Tom said. "Ever since I was eight years old. This will be our fifth trip in five years!"

Kevin said, "My family usually goes to an amusement park for the week before school starts. This is going to be way more fun. I'm excited."

A moment later, the pickup truck turned off the dirt road into a small, dusty clearing.

"Here we are," said Tom's dad. He opened his door and stepped down, out of the truck. "You boys give me a hand with the unloading."

"This is it?" Kevin asked Tom in a whisper.

He was expecting to see beautiful scenery. Tom had mentioned a huge mountain and a big lake. He had said that the lake was smooth as glass and full of fish.

But Tom's dad had parked the pickup in a parking lot next to a several other trucks, SUVs, and station wagons. The only things to see were a few lame-looking pines and an outhouse.

So far, Kevin thought, staring out the truck's window, *the amusement park sounds better than a camping trip.*

Tom saw the confused look on his friend's face. "This is just where we park the truck," he told Kevin. "The good stuff is still coming."

He glanced out the back window at his dad, who had removed the tarp from the truck bed and was starting to unload. "Let's help my dad unload," Tom said. "Then we'll have a short hike to where we'll pitch the tents."

* * *

Kevin tugged at the shoulder straps of his pack. He'd never hiked before, but it wasn't so bad. If not for carrying the heavy pack and walking on the dirt path, it would be pretty much the same as plain old walking.

"Doing okay, Kevin?" Tom's dad asked. He was walking in front, leading the way.

Kevin called up to him, "Yes, I'm doing fine, Mr. Peck."

Tom's dad laughed. "Kevin, while we're out here in the wild, just us guys, no more of this 'Mr.' stuff," he said. "Call me Ben, all right?"

"Okay, um, Ben," Kevin replied. It felt weird to call his friend's dad by his first name.

"We're almost there," Tom said, walking next to Kevin. "Right after this part we'll see our spot."

"You call this a short hike?" Kevin asked. He wiped some sweat off his face.

Tom laughed. "This is nothing," he said. "Sometimes when my dad and I come up here, we hike all day, just enjoying the forest and the mountains."

The boys followed Ben up a narrow slope. Kevin noticed that Tom's dad used the roots that stuck out of the ground as steps to climb up.

Tom followed his dad's footsteps exactly as he headed up the hill. "If you don't use the roots, the ground will be too slippery," he said to Kevin. "You'll be flat on your butt in no time."

Kevin did his best to follow the others, but he had to steady himself with his hands on the ground too. "I'll make it," he grunted.

"Just wait," Ben called down from the top. "After this week, you'll be a regular mountain man!"

Kevin reached the top. The three walked for another few minutes. Soon, they reached a clearing at the top of the hill.

"Wow," Kevin said as he looked around.

"Great spot, huh?" Tom said.

Kevin nodded. In one direction, down a hill, he could see the smooth lake Tom had told him about. A fine mist was gliding across the lake's surface. The glassy lake reflected the small, sharp mountains around it.

Kevin had never seen anything like it, at least not in person. He'd seen this sort of thing on postcards, and in movies. But he lived in the city. He'd never seen something like this in real life.

Turning around, Kevin saw a mountain peak that was higher than all the others. It stood over the wild like a king guarding his kingdom.

Kevin whistled. "What's that mountain called?" he asked.

"That's the one I told you about the other day," Tom said. "The volcano."

"I can't believe it's a real, live volcano," Kevin said in awe. "That's so cool. Is it dangerous?"

"No, don't worry about it," Ben said. "We're safe. It's dormant."

"That means it's sleeping," Tom explained. "It hasn't erupted in, like, a hundred years."

Ben put his arm around his son's shoulders. "Exactly," he said. "There's nothing to worry about. Now let's get these tents set up!"

CHAPTER 2

TOTALLY SAFE

After a hard day of setting up the campsite and collecting firewood, the cool night was a relief. The boys and Ben sat around a campfire.

"This is the life, right, boys?" Ben asked. He leaned back against a rock and blew into his metal mug. "Hot chocolate, a campfire, and lots of stars."

. Tom and Kevin looked up at the sky. It was the starriest night Kevin had ever seen.

"It's amazing," Kevin said. "You sure can't see this many stars back in town."

"There are too many lights in the city," Tom said. "That makes it hard to see any but the brightest stars."

Kevin looked around and above him. Part of the sky was totally black, without a star to be seen. "The volcano blocks a lot of the sky, doesn't it?" he said.

"Well, it is huge," Ben replied. Then he yawned. "Well, boys," he added, "I'm pretty tired out from that hike. At my age, all it takes is a little walk and some hot milk, and I'm ready to sleep."

Tom and Kevin laughed. "Okay, Dad," Tom said. "Is it all right if we stay up and talk for a while? I'm not ready to go to bed yet."

Ben nodded, but had a stern look on his face. "It's all right," he said, "but don't be up too late. We should get up early to go fishing in the morning. We have to catch our breakfast!"

"Okay," Tom said.

"We'll go to bed soon," Kevin added.

Ben got up and stretched. "Good night, boys," he said. "I'll wake you both up at dawn."

Ben kicked off his hiking boots and crawled into his tent. The boys sat quietly for a while, just watching the night.

"Have you ever caught any fish?" Kevin asked.

"Of course I have," Tom replied. "Lots. We have to catch fish to survive out here in the wild."

"Wait a second. Didn't we bring any food?" Kevin asked.

"Yeah, we did," Tom said. He laughed. "We always bring some cans of beans or some chili or something. But we've never had to open a single can. We always catch a ton of fish. The only other food we actually use is the coffee — for Dad — and the milk and hot chocolate."

"I've never even gone fishing before," Kevin said. "Do you think I'll be able to catch anything?"

Tom nodded. "Sure you will," he said. "We've got a nice rod for you to use, and good bait. And it's easy to learn to fish. Dad and I have fished so many times on this lake, it's a breeze for us. We know exactly how to catch fish here."

"Okay," Kevin said. "I don't want to starve, or have to eat beans all week."

Tom laughed. "Well, even if you don't catch anything, don't worry," he said. "We won't make you eat beans all week."

Kevin laughed and leaned back. He looked up at the dark mountain towering over them. It was a little scary. Kevin didn't feel like laughing while he was looking at the huge volcano, even if it was asleep.

"Should we be this close to a volcano?" Kevin asked, staring up at the mountain. "Once I read about this huge volcano in ancient Italy that wiped out a whole city."

Tom reminded him, "It's dormant."

"Right, I know, it's sleeping," Kevin replied. "Still, it's pretty freaky to be this close."

"You'll get used to it," Tom said. "The park has rules about how close you can go to that mountain. Dad and I always follow those rules."

"It looks pretty close to me," Kevin said.

"It looks close because it's so big," Tom replied. "We're actually, like, twenty miles away."

"Twenty miles?" Kevin asked, surprised. He realized that would take eighty laps around the school's track. "That's pretty far."

Tom took a sip of his cocoa. "Yeah," he said. "Anything closer than ten miles is called the red zone. No one is allowed in there. Out this far, we're totally safe."

CHAPTER 3

SLEEPING IN

The sun rose behind the smaller mountains around the lake. Ben stood over the glowing embers of the campfire and stretched.

"Sure is good to be up here again," he muttered to himself.

He took a deep breath and let out a big sigh. Then he poured himself a cup of hot coffee.

Ben enjoyed the quiet of early mornings in the mountains. He smelled the pine and fresh air. He even thought he could smell the cool water of the lake and the cold peaks of the mountains surrounding them.

Sitting on a rock, he took a few sips of his coffee. He watched the steam as it floated away from his mug. For a few moments, he watched the sun rise higher over the lake. Then he found his backpack.

Ben dug around in his backpack for a few minutes, gathering the supplies they'd need for the fishing trip. After a little while, he'd assembled three fishing poles and sorted through his tackle box. Then he lifted the flap to the boys' tent.

"Boys," Ben said, sticking his head in. "Hey, Tom. Are you awake?"

Tom quietly muttered something into his pillow.

"Sorry, I didn't catch that," Ben said with a laugh. "Time to get up and catch some breakfast."

The boys turned over in their sleeping bags, but they didn't really wake up. "Ready to go, Kevin?" Ben said. "Will this be your first time fishing?"

Kevin didn't answer. He just let out a little snore and went right on snoozing.

Ben grabbed Tom's foot and gave it a wiggle. "He still has his boots on, I see," Ben said to himself. "Come on, Tom," he added louder. "It's fishing time. Up and at 'em."

"Dad," Tom finally replied. "Can't we just sleep a little longer?"

Ben shook his head. "Don't think so," he said. "The sun is already higher than I'd like for fishing."

"But we were up real late," Tom said, struggling to open his eyes. "Kevin's never been camping before. He had a lot of questions, so we stayed up talking."

"Didn't I tell you boys not to stay up so late?" Ben asked. Tom could tell he was a little annoyed.

"Yes, Dad," Tom replied. "But I've never had a friend on a camping trip before. We got carried away."

Ben sighed loudly. "Well, this fishing needs to be done if we're going to have anything to eat. I sure don't want three meals of canned beans today," he said. He waited, but Tom didn't say anything.

"If you boys are going to join me, you need to come along now," Ben said. "If you want to sleep in, I'll go fishing alone."

"We'd like to sleep in, Dad," Tom said. "I'm sorry. We won't stay up late tonight, I promise. And we'll all go fishing tomorrow morning."

"Okay," Ben said. "I'll head to the lake. If you boys feel like joining me, you know where to find me."

He pulled his head out of the tent. Tom heard his dad gather up his pole and tackle and walk off. Tom hoped his dad wasn't too mad. It was just too hard to get up. After only a few seconds, he fell back asleep.

CHAPTER 4

IT'S WAKING UP!

Tom was in a deep sleep when he felt something shaking him. He thought it was his dad shaking him again. He would have sworn it had only been a few minutes since his dad had left to go fishing. He couldn't be back already!

"Dad," Tom said. "Go fishing without us, please? We'll come down to the lake later." Then Tom rolled over to try to get back to sleep.

But still, he felt someone shaking him awake. "Kevin, is that you?" he muttered, still half asleep. "Leave me alone!"

Kevin didn't reply, but the shaking stopped. Tom smiled to himself and tried to fall back asleep.

Kevin woke up. He wiggled his toes. He realized he'd fallen asleep with his boots on.

"Great," he mumbled to himself. "My mom is not going to be happy if this sleeping bag has mud and dirt inside it from my boots."

Kevin carefully pulled his feet out of the sleeping bag and crawled out of the tent. He pulled the sleeping bag after him and stood up to shake it out. Sure enough, dirt came pouring out.

"Darn it," he said.

"What's wrong?" Tom called from inside the tent. "I'm trying to sleep."

"Nothing," Kevin called back. "I just fell asleep with my boots on, and now there's lots of dirt inside my sleeping bag."

"So did I," Tom replied. "Who cares?"

"My mom will, for one," Kevin said. "She'll kill me!"

Suddenly, the ground shook. Kevin nearly fell over. "Whoa," he whispered. "What's going on?"

"Quit shaking me!" Tom called from the tent.

"That wasn't me!" Kevin yelled back. "I'm not even inside the tent."

"What was it, then?" Tom yelled.

"I don't know. You better come out here," Kevin called back.

Tom crawled out from the tent and stood up next to his friend. "What's going on?"

Kevin pointed past Tom toward the big mountain. Tom turned and saw a dark gray cloud surrounding the mountaintop.

The ground continued to rumble. It shook lightly at first, but then it moved enough that Tom and Kevin both had trouble staying on their feet.

"That dormant volcano?" Kevin said. "I think it's waking up!"

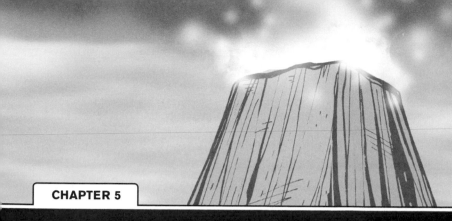

CHAPTER 5

THE CLOUD OF ASH

"Dad!" Tom screamed through the morning mountain air. "Dad, where are you?"

"Where is he?" Kevin asked over the sound of the shaking earth. "I thought he was waiting for us."

"He must still be fishing," Tom replied. "He woke me up at dawn, but I said we wanted to sleep more."

A loud boom came from the volcano. The boys looked up. They saw another big cloud of ash blow into the sky.

"Your dad went fishing alone?" Kevin asked.

Tom nodded. "I wish we'd gone with him," he said. He looked at his feet.

"Don't worry about that now," Kevin said. "Let's go to the lake and find him."

The two boys rushed along the path toward the lake. As they ran, the earth shook. Kevin fell down.

"Kevin!" Tom called. "You have to stay on your feet!" He ran back to Kevin and reached out his hand.

"I'm trying," Kevin replied. After he got up, he looked down at his jeans. They were muddy and torn at the knees.

"Are you okay?" Tom asked.

Kevin nodded. "I think so. Let's keep going," he said. The boys took off running again.

"The lake is just a little farther down this hill," Tom called back.

Soon, Kevin spotted the lake. It wasn't smooth like glass this morning. Waves were crashing on it. And there was no sign of Tom's dad.

"He's not here!" Tom yelled. "He must have gone back to the campsite!"

Just as the boys were about to head back, there was another bang. It was the loudest one yet.

The sound made Kevin jump. He stopped and turned to face the erupting volcano.

"Look!" Kevin shouted. He grabbed Tom's arm and pointed back at the volcano.

Tom turned to look. The great black cloud around the volcano was turning red, orange, and yellow. Flames and lava spewed into the sky. The cloud of ash and smoke got bigger and bigger.

As they watched, the cloud of ash began to spread out. Then it started to roll down the mountainside toward them.

"We have to find shelter," Tom said. "Now!"

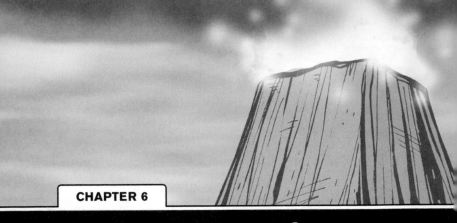

CHAPTER 6

THE CAVE

"I know a place we can go," Tom said. The earth continued to shake as Tom led Kevin away from the lake.

"Shouldn't we go toward the campsite?" Kevin said, worried. "I mean, shouldn't we try to find your dad?"

Tom shook his head. "It's more important to get shelter from that," he said. He pointed at the rolling black cloud. It was moving toward them quickly.

"It might just look like a cloud of smoke that would make you cough a little," Tom added, "but it's actually super hot. It could kill you or leave you burned for the rest of your life!"

"Wait a second. What about your dad?" Kevin said.

"He'll be okay," Tom said. "He knows everything there is to know about surviving up here. Come on. Let's go!"

Kevin and Tom ran through the woods. Kevin couldn't believe Tom knew his way around so well.

"How do you know where to go?" Kevin asked.

"I found a good spot a few years ago when I was exploring," Tom said. "It will be just what we need."

The ground was still shaking. The boys kept running. Kevin could smell the scorched earth and trees. The burning cloud was getting closer.

"Here!" Tom yelled. He jumped off a small hill just in front of Kevin.

Kevin ran to the edge and looked over, but he didn't see Tom anywhere. "Where are you?" Kevin shouted.

"Here!" Tom replied. Suddenly, his head popped out near Kevin's feet. "There's a cave in this hill!"

Kevin hopped off the hill. He crawled into the cave with Tom.

They crawled all the way to the back of the cave. There, the ceiling was a little higher and it was cool and damp. But it was a tight fit.

"You think we'll be okay in here?" Kevin asked. He wasn't sure a small hole in the ground would protect them from a powerful volcano.

Tom nodded. "We should be," he said. "The cloud is coming from the west, and the cave entrance is facing east. The cloud should roll right over us. It won't be able to come into the cave, since it's going the other way. So I think the hill should protect us pretty well."

They sat for a few minutes. Kevin tried to brush some of the mud off his jeans.

"Can you smell that?" Tom asked.

Kevin nodded. "It smells terrible," he said. "And I can feel it now, too. It's getting hot. It feels like when my mom opens the oven to check on a cake."

Tom gasped. "Look!" he said, pointing out the mouth of the little cave.

Dark gray ashes were flowing past the cave. Little fires were starting everywhere just outside the cave's opening. Because of the smoke and flames, Tom and Kevin couldn't see more than a foot past the cave entrance.

After a few moments, the ashes settled. The ground stopped shaking. Kevin thought it looked safe.

"Can we climb out now?" Kevin asked. "I think it's over." He started to crawl toward the cave's entrance, but Tom grabbed his arm.

"Wait," Tom said. "Watch this." He pulled a scrap of paper from his pocket and tossed it out of the cave.

It hit the ashes and began to turn brown on the edges. Soon it was glowing orange.

"We have to wait," Tom said.

Kevin nodded and stared out at the burning scrap of paper. *That could have been me!* he thought nervously.

CHAPTER 7

WAITING

Tom and Kevin sat in the cave with their shirt collars pulled up over their mouths and noses. The taste and smell of the volcano's ash was awful.

"Is it poisonous?" Kevin asked quietly. His voice was muffled. He had his eyes closed tight, because the air was making them water. "The ashes and stuff, I mean," he added. "If we breathe them, are they poisonous?"

"I think so," Tom said. "My dad told me that volcano fumes are poisonous. But don't worry. I don't think we're going to breathe in too much of it."

By the time the ash seemed cool enough, they had been sitting in the cave for hours. They'd been breathing through their shirts and keeping their eyes closed.

"Think it's safe now?" Kevin asked.

Tom threw another scrap of paper out of the cave. He squinted out the cave mouth and watched. The paper didn't burn.

"It's not hot enough to burn the paper," Tom replied, "but it's probably still hot. It might burn us a little."

Kevin took a deep breath through his shirt. Then he started to crawl out into the ash.

"Ouch!" he said when his hands touched the ground. "It is still hot!" He got to his feet and waved his hands to cool them.

"I can't believe how deep it is," Tom said as he crawled out and stood up next to Kevin. The layer of ashes reached up to their knees, but the ashes weren't hot enough to burn through their clothes.

Tom and Kevin looked around. Everything was covered with ash. Some trees had fallen over. Everything looked totally different.

"You still know how to get back to the campsite, right?" Kevin asked.

Tom looked at him and slowly shook his head. "No," Tom said. "I have no idea."

CHAPTER 8

A DIFFERENT PLANET

"Can you tell which way the lake is?" Kevin asked.

Tom looked around. "Well, the cave is right here," he said, "so the lake must be that way." He pointed past the cave mouth to the west. "But everything looks so different," he added. "I don't know if I could find the trail."

"We have to try," Kevin said.

"I know," Tom said. "Let's go."

They headed off in the direction Tom had pointed. Tom led the way.

"Does any of this look familiar?" Kevin asked as they walked.

Tom shook his head. "Nothing looks familiar," he replied. "I feel like I'm on a different planet!"

"It looks like pictures of the moon I've seen," Kevin replied.

Tom nodded. "Or a scene from a movie," he said. "One that's about the end of the world."

"It shouldn't be too hard to find a lake," Kevin said.

Tom shrugged. "It might be," he said. "All those ashes are probably floating on the water. It might look more like a gray field now, instead of a lake."

"We might not know we found the lake until we fall in the water!" Kevin said.

Tom chuckled. "That's true," he said. "But at least then we'll know we found it."

It seemed to Kevin like they'd been walking for hours. Finally, he heard something. It sounded like a voice. "Hey," he said, grabbing Tom's wrist. "Did you hear that?"

Tom held his breath and listened as hard as he could.

"Tom!" the voice called. It seemed far away. "Tom! Kevin! Where are you guys?"

"It's Dad!" Tom cried. He and Kevin started to run.

Ben kept calling to them. His voice seemed to be getting closer. "Boys!" he called.

Finally, Tom spotted his dad on a hill.

Tom ran faster. Kevin squinted and followed his friend. Together they ran toward the slope, waving their arms.

"Tom!" Ben shouted as he spotted them. "Kevin! You're all right! Thank goodness!"

He ran down the side of the hill and grabbed both boys in his arms. "I'm so glad to see you two," Ben said. "Are you okay?"

Tom nodded. "We found shelter," he said. "I knew a good place to hide."

"That's my boy," Ben said. He gave Tom another hug.

"Kevin burned his hands a little, I think," Tom added.

Kevin held his hands out to Ben. They were red. Kevin had almost forgotten that he'd burned them.

"They don't look too bad," Ben said. "Do they hurt?"

Kevin shook his head.

"And your feet are okay?" Ben asked.

Kevin looked down at his shoes. "Good thing we fell asleep with our hiking boots on," he said, "or that would have been a much tougher hike!"

"What happened to you, Dad?" Tom asked. "We came running to the lake when the eruption started."

"I was on my way back to you!" Ben said. "As soon as the ground started rumbling, I headed back to camp. When I got there, your tent was empty."

"We were headed for the lake!" Kevin said.

"That's what I thought," Ben replied. "So I went back to the lake. When the ash cloud came rolling over, I dove underwater and stayed there until the ashes settled. That only took a minute. Then I had to wade around until the ash on the shore had cooled down enough."

The boys looked at Ben's jeans. They were wet and muddy and covered with ash. In a few places, it looked like they had been burned all the way through.

"Are you hurt at all, Dad?" Tom asked nervously.

Ben shook his head. "I have a few little burns on my legs," he said. "But I'm fine. I'm just so glad to see that you boys are okay." He put his arms around Tom and Kevin's shoulders.

Then he added, "I hope this never happens again, but if it does, remember to stay at the campsite, especially when it's on high ground, like ours is. Okay?"

"Okay," the boys said.

"And one more thing," Ben said. "From now on, I hope you'll always sleep with your hiking boots on!"

Kevin laughed. "I thought my mom would be mad at me for getting mud in my sleeping bag," he said. "But now I'm pretty sure she won't mind at all."

CHAPTER 9

SAFE

Tom, Kevin, and Ben walked toward the parking lot. They followed Ben's compass.

"It shouldn't be too far," Ben said as they walked. "However, I don't know if we'll be able to drive out of here through all the ash."

The forest was quiet. Kevin could hardly believe that just a few hours earlier, a volcano had erupted.

Suddenly, the silence was shattered again. A booming sound, like a huge motor in the sky, tore through the forest.

"What is that?" Kevin shouted over the sound.

"Look up there!" Tom yelled, pointing over their heads. A blue helicopter was hovering over the park.

"Down here!" Kevin shouted. Ben and Tom shouted too. They all waved their arms.

"We see you," a voice called down from the helicopter's loudspeaker. "We are going to lower a ladder for you."

Ben turned to Kevin. "Do you think you can climb with those burns on your hands?" Ben asked.

"I'll be okay," Kevin replied.

Soon a rope ladder was dangling in front of him. Gusts of wind from the helicopter's blades pushed Kevin as he grabbed the ladder.

The ash was stirred by the wind. The air around them turned gray. Ash flew into Kevin's eyes, hair, and ears.

"Hold on tight!" yelled a voice from the helicopter.

Kevin struggled his way up the ladder. Though the helicopter was hovering pretty still, it was still making the ladder sway and shake. And even though the burns on his hands weren't too bad, it did hurt to hold on to the rungs.

I can do this, Kevin thought. He glanced down at Tom and Ben, who were looking up at him.

Then Kevin raised his head. He looked at the man waiting for him at the top of the ladder.

"There you go, son," the man was shouting down to him. "You're nearly at the top!"

Finally, Kevin could see the man clearly. He was wearing a green uniform and helmet. As soon as Kevin was within the man's reach, the man grabbed Kevin's armpits and pulled him into the helicopter.

"You're all right," the man said. "Sit here." He pointed toward an empty seat behind him. Kevin sat down and put on his seatbelt.

Soon Tom and Ben climbed aboard too. They sat next to Kevin on the rear bench of the helicopter.

"We're going to fly the three of you straight to a hospital," the man in green said after he pulled up the ladder. The helicopter was already speeding toward the nearest town. "When you're feeling healthy enough, someone will help you come back for your truck . . . when it's safe."

Ben shook the man's hand and said, "Thank you."

The man in the green uniform smiled. He went to the front of the helicopter and sat next to the pilot.

Kevin leaned back in his seat. He took a few deep breaths. Then he glanced out the helicopter's window. They'd already left the area that had been covered in ash. A pine forest and some mountain lakes were below them.

Tom nudged him. "I swear, this won't happen next year," Tom said. "But maybe instead of camping we should plan to go to an amusement park or something."

Kevin smiled. "I don't know," he said. "I don't think any amusement park ride will be able to compare to this!"

ABOUT THE AUTHOR

Eric Stevens lives in St. Paul, Minnesota. He is studying to become a middle-school English teacher. Some of his favorite things include pizza, playing video games, watching cooking shows on TV, riding his bike, and trying new restaurants. Some of his least favorite things include olives and shoveling snow.

ABOUT THE ILLUSTRATOR

When Sean Tiffany was growing up, he lived on a small island off the coast of Maine. Every day, from sixth grade until he graduated from high school, he had to take a boat to get to school. When Sean isn't working on his art, he works on a multimedia project called "OilCan Drive," which combines music and art. He has a pet cactus named Jim.

GLOSSARY

ash (ASH)—the powder that remains after something has been burned

cave (KAYV)—a large hole underground or in the side of a hill or cliff

clearing (KLEER-ing)—an area of forest or woods from which trees have been removed

dormant (DOR-muhnt)—a dormant volcano is not active at present, but could erupt again

embers (EM-burz)—the hot remains of a fire

erupt (i-RUHPT)—when a volcano erupts, it throws out rocks, hot ashes, and lava with great force

familiar (fuh-MIL-yur)—easily recognized

lava (LA-vuh)—hot, liquid rock that pours out of a volcano

poisonous (POI-zuhn-uss)—if something is poisonous, it can kill or harm someone

scenery (SEE-nur-ee)—the natural countryside of an area, such as trees, hills, mountains, and lakes

FIVE FAMOUS VOLCANOES

Volcanoes are some of the world's most amazing wonders. Here are five of the most famous:

Krakatau, Indonesia: This volcano's most damaging eruption was in 1883. About 36,000 people on nearby islands died. For three years, ash from the blast caused brilliant red sunsets worldwide.

Mount Vesuvius, Italy: This volcano is famous for its eruption in the year 79. The ancient city of Pompeii disappeared under ashes and stone. Today, workers have uncovered only three-fourths of the city.

Mauna Loa, Hawaii: This is the world's largest volcano. Its peak is at 13,677 feet. Back in 1855–1856, Mauna Loa erupted for 18 months.

Mount Fuji, Japan: Tourists love to climb this symbol of Japan. It hasn't erupted since 1707, and the risk of eruption remains low.

Mount Saint Helens, Washington: This volcano last erupted in 1980. Fifty-seven people were killed. Ashes and gases destroyed nearly 150 square miles of forest. More than 185 miles of roadway were also damaged.

DISCUSSION QUESTIONS

1. What other stories do you know about volcanoes? Talk about movies, books, and TV shows that have given you information about volcanoes.

2. Kevin and Tom hide in a cave to stay out of the way of the lava and ash. What would have happened if there wasn't a cave there? What else could they have done to stay safe?

3. Kevin's family goes to an amusement park every summer. Tom and his dad go camping. What are some other things that families do during the summer? Talk about ways to have fun during summer vacation.

WRITING PROMPTS

1. Have you ever gone camping? Write about your camping trip. If you haven't gone camping, write about a camping trip you'd like to take.

2. Tom brings Kevin on the camping trip with his dad because they're best friends. Who is your best friend? Write about that person. Make sure to include some of the reasons that you like that person.

3. At the end of this book, Kevin and Tom talk about whether they'll go camping again next year. Write a story about what happens the next year when Kevin and Tom go on a trip. Do they go camping or do something else? Where do they go? What do they do?

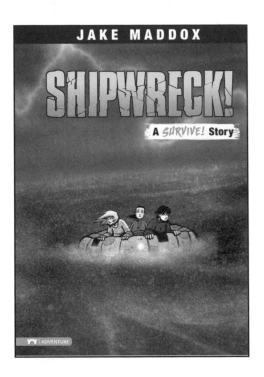

When their whale-watching trip goes horribly wrong, Skylar, Gabby, and Miles find themselves on an inflatable raft in the middle of the ocean. They must spend three treacherous days on the waves, hoping desperately for help to arrive. Will they survive, or are they lost at sea forever?

BY JAKE MADDOX

Owen and Gray are stranded in the middle of a raging blizzard. Once the storm subsides, the boys decide to try to find their way back to civilization. Can they make it safely home, or will the frozen elements become too much for them to handle?

INTERNET SITES

Do you want to know more about subjects related to this book? Or are you interested in learning about other topics? Then check out FactHound, a fun, easy way to find Internet sites.

Our investigative staff has already sniffed out great sites for you!

Here's how to use FactHound:

1. Visit *www.facthound.com*

2. Select your grade level.

3. To learn more about subjects related to this book, type in the book's ISBN number: **9781434212085**.

4. Click the **Fetch It** button.

FactHound will fetch the best Internet sites for you!